INSPIRED BY
JAZZY AND J.J.

MOMMY LOVES
YOU

Snookumpie Story Time

We hope you enjoy this
book written by our
dear friend ! Welcome
to the world!
♥ Shelly i Christian
Schmidt

2022

1 *angry **a**lligator swung his tail at the

*Angry- Feeling upset or annoyed

2 *beaming beetles who were getting chased by the

*Beaming- Shining brightly

3 *chubby **C**ats who like to play tricks on the

*Chubby- Plump and round

4 *dalmatian dogs who enjoy playing hide and seek with the

*Dalmatian- A type of spotted dog

5 *enormous **e**lephants that live next to the

*Enormous-Huge

6 *funky frogs who scare the

*Funky= Smelly or having rythm

7 *generous gorillas that always share their food with the

8 *happy hedgehogs whose best friends are the

friends are the

*Happy-Feeling joy

9 *intelligent iguanas that like to paint with the

*Intelligent-Smart

10 *jaunty jaguars who teach an art class to the

*Jaunty: Fashionable and stylish

11 *kempt Kangaroos that frighten the

*kempt, eat and study.

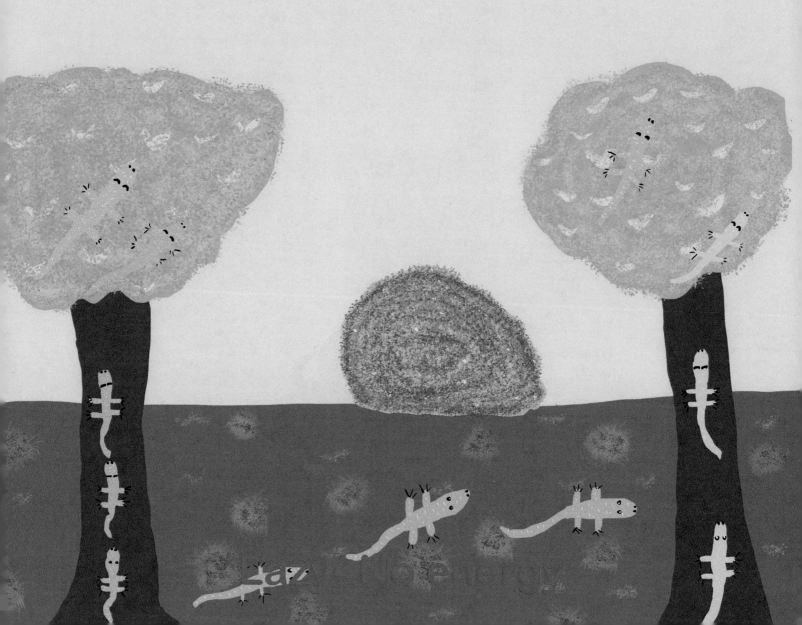

12 *lazy lizards who were sleeping in the tree next to the

13 *meditating **m**onkeys, and one fell and bumped his head on

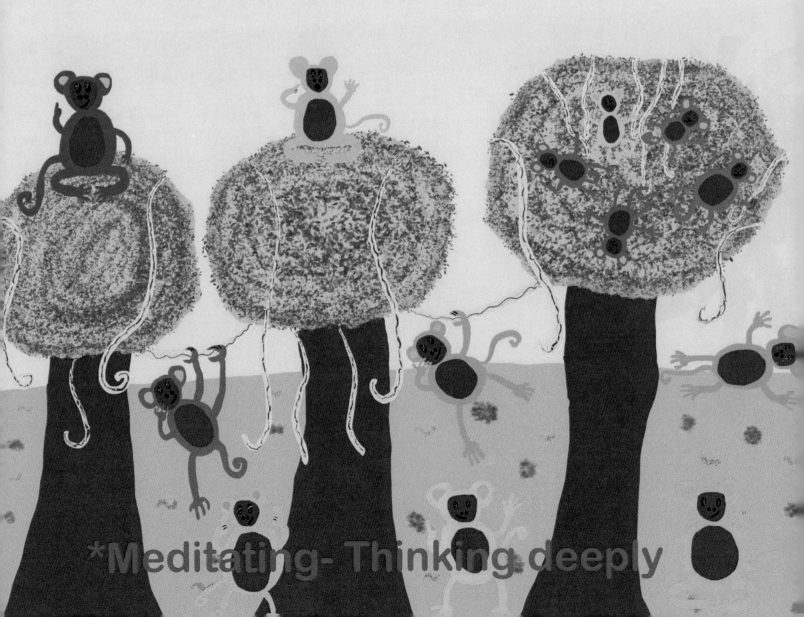

*Meditating- Thinking deeply

14 *noisy **n**umbats who were watching

*Noisy- Making a lot of noise

15 *orange Ostriches getting ready for their run with the

*Orange: A type of color

START

16 *pacey Parrots whose adoptive siblings are the

*Pacey- Moving fast

FINISH

17 *questioning quails who are doctors and some of their patients are the

are the

*Questioning- Asking

18 *rugged rabbits that have alot of baby bunnies so they have

*Rugged- Strong

19 *sweet **S**nake nannies who also watch

sweet- Nice

20 *tiny turtles whose parents are on vacation with

*Tiny- Small

21*unique Unicorn fishes that sometime travel with

*Unique- Being the only one of its kind

22 *vigorous Vaquitas who have

*Vigorous- Having alot of strength and energy

23 *whiny Whale cousins that sometimes get stuck in the sand so

*Whiny- Complaing in a high pitch sound

24 *xanthic **X**erus squirrels always figure out a plan to get them out with help from the

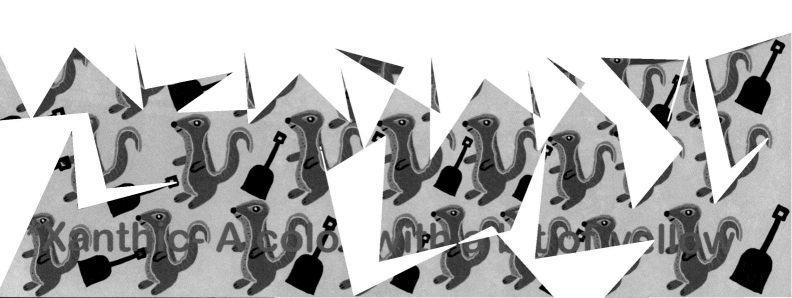

Xanthic: A color with a lot of yellow

25 *yodeling yaks that have music class with

*Yodeling: A type of singing voice

26 *zappy Zebras that have

*Zappy - Lively and energetic

27 zamias

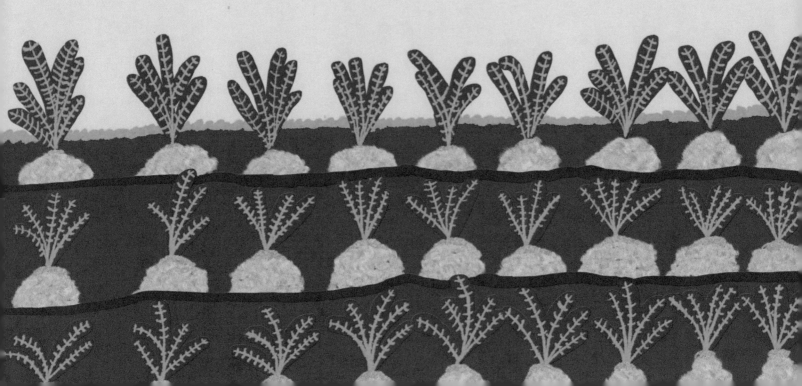

28 zucchini

29 zinnias and

30 zz plants growing in their garden.

Made in the USA
Coppell, TX
17 June 2021